Motorcycles: Made for Speed!™

COOL BIKES

Connor Dayton

PowerKiDS
press™
New York

Published in 2007 by The Rosen Publishing Group, Inc.
29 East 21st Street, New York, NY 10010

First Edition

Editor: Jennifer Way
Book Design: Ginny Chu
Layout Design: Kate Laczynski
Photo Researcher: Sam Cha

Photo Credits: Cover, pp. 1, 5, 7, 13 © Getty Images; pp. 9, 11, 15, 17, 19, 21, 23 © www.shutterstock.com.

Library of Congress Cataloging-in-Publication Data

Dayton, Connor.
   Cool bikes / Connor Dayton. — 1st ed.
      p. cm. — (Motorcycles--made for speed)
   Includes index.
   ISBN-13: 978-1-4042-3655-4 (library binding)
   ISBN-10: 1-4042-3655-4 (library binding)
   1. Motorcycles—Juvenile literature. I. Title.

TL440.15.D3876 2007
629.227'5—dc22

                                        2006024587

Manufactured in the United States of America

Contents

Cool bikes can be almost any type of motorcycle. They sometimes have a **design** that has never been seen before.

This is a new kind of motorcycle that runs on **electricity**. Most other motorcycles run on gas.

Some bikes are cool because they are old. These are called **antique** bikes.

This small motorcycle is called a minibike.

This motorcycle has only one wheel! It is called a monocycle.

13

Some people add finishing touches to their bikes. The owner of this bike put a furry covering on it.

Sometimes people give their bikes **custom** paint jobs. This bike has been painted to look like a zebra.

Some motorcycles are built with things that are not often used to build bikes. This bike is covered in leather!

People can add things to their bikes to make them more fun to ride. This bike has a sidecar.

21

People also add places to store their things on their bikes. This can make taking long trips much easier.

Glossary

antique (an-TEEK) Made a long time ago.

custom (KUS-tum) Made in a certain way for a person.

design (dih-ZYN) The plan or the form of something.

electricity (ih-lek-TRIH-suh-tee) Power that makes light, heat, or movement.

Index

Web Sites

Due to the changing nature of Internet links, PowerKids Press has developed an online list of Web sites related to this book. This site is updated regularly. Please use this link to access the list:

www.powerkidslinks.com/motor/coolbikes/